Nick, the No Good, Icky Tick

Story by Karen Gloyer

Illustration by Maryana Kachmar

with an Afterword by Kenneth B. Singleton, M.D., M.P.H.,
Lyme disease specialist and author of The Lyme Disease Solution

BELLE ISLE BOOKS
www.belleislebooks.com

ISBN: 978-1-939930-83-5

Library of Congress Control Number: 2016956791

BELLE ISLE BOOKS
www.belleislebooks.com

I dedicate this book
to my family, friends and doctors
who continue to help me through the healing process.

Once upon a time in the wild wild woods,
there lived all sorts of creatures.

There were inchworms, deer, ticks and bear. The wild wild woods had them all!

It was a nice summer day when Abby's family decided to go for a hike in the wild wild woods. Abby was set to go. She had her backpack... her Mom and Dad... and best of all, her favorite four-footed friend, Chowser!

Abby hiked in fields of long, thick, green grass.

She hiked in the forest where
bushes and big trees grew.

Abby even saw a deer that day!

The same day that Abby was hiking, Nick was taking a walk, too.

Nick, you see, was a no good, icky tick.
He had big eyes and black legs.

Nick set out for a walk in the meadow.
He was ready for a wild ride.

Suddenly, he saw the same deer.
Ah ha! Quick! Nick hopped on the deer.
His adventure was about to get exciting!

Nick held on tight as the deer raced through the long, green grass. They ran through the woods. They ran and ran!

Finally, the deer laid down
on a soft bed of leaves.

All of this adventure made Nick hungry.

Do you know what icky ticks eat? They eat blood... So Nick nibbled on the deer for food.

With his belly full, Nick wanted to rest, so he jumped off the deer and into some bushes. He found a cozy spot and curled up for a nap.

Uh oh!

Nick, the no good, icky tick
began to feel... sick!

Nick got hot.

His body began to ache.

His black-tick legs began to hurt.

Just then, Nick the icky, sick tick saw a dog pass by.
Nick jumped on him for an easy ride home.

Do you know who that dog was?

It was Abby's dog, Chowser! Nick held tight
to Chowser as they walked back through the
woods… jumped in the car…and headed home.

Whew! Nick was relieved. He curled up and fell fast asleep.

When Nick woke up, they were at Abby's house. Nick was still sick and wobbly on his little black legs, but he wanted to look around. He walked slowly from Chowser... right over to Abby. Nick, the no good, icky tick, took a seat on the girl's back.

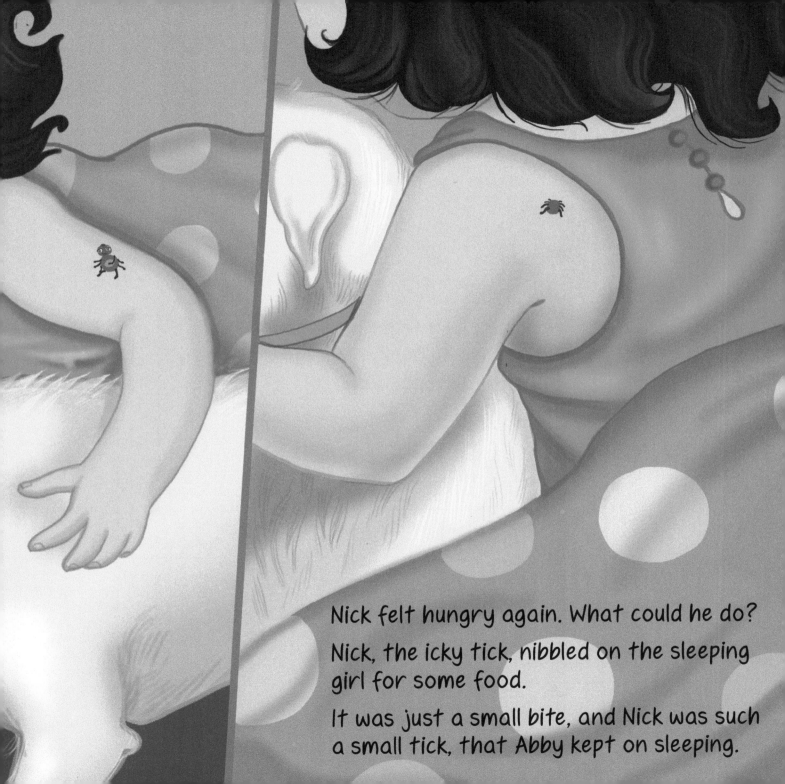

Nick felt hungry again. What could he do?

Nick, the icky tick, nibbled on the sleeping girl for some food.

It was just a small bite, and Nick was such a small tick, that Abby kept on sleeping.

Nick, the icky tick was so small that no one even saw him. He hid on Abby's back for several days.

Then, one day at bath time, Abby's Mom saw a small black dot. She said, "Oh no, you have a tick! Let me get that off!"

A few weeks later,
Abby started feeling sick.

She was tired, her head hurt,
and she was hot with fever.

Her arms and legs hurt.

Her knees and elbows swelled.

What was wrong with Abby?

Why was she so sick?
Her Mom and Dad were worried.

Then, a clue!

Abby got a strange rash on her skin.
It was right where Nick, the no good, icky tick had been!

Abby's mom took her to the doctor.

The doctor said Abby was sick with Lyme disease.

Lyme disease... How could this be?

It turns out that Nick, the no good, icky tick carried Lyme disease to Abby.

It started with that deer!
When Nick bit the deer for food, he got sick with Lyme disease.

When the sick tick bit the girl, Abby got Lyme disease, too.
That is why Abby became so ill.

Trace Nick's path to Abby.

But, good news!
Abby took medicine so now
she feels much better.

Now, when Abby and Chowser go for walks… guess what?
They know to always look for ticks when they get home.

Look carefully…

Lots of great adventures, but no more icky, sick ticks!

A MESSAGE TO PARENTS ABOUT LYME DISEASE

Lyme disease is an infection that results from a tick bite. It has become the number one vector-borne disease in the United States (i.e. transmitted by insects or bugs). The CDC states that while over 25,000-30,000 cases are reported annually, the actual number is likely 10 times greater. Most doctors on the frontlines of Lyme clinical care believe the actual number is more like 25 times the CDC's reported case number. It is rare to meet a person who doesn't know someone who has had Lyme disease or is currently suffering from the effects of this disease.

Lyme disease is called "the new great imitator" because of its ability to look like so many other diseases and conditions. It is frequently misdiagnosed, as the classic "bull's eye rash" is often absent and the blood test is unreliably negative. Lyme is taking its toll in terms of human misery in the United States and in many other countries. When Lyme is combined with other tick-borne infections (i.e. Babesia, Bartonella, Mycoplasma, Ehrlichia, Anaplasma, and Rocky Mountain Spotted Fever, to name a few), it becomes especially problematic, especially when a tick may pass on several different infections during a single bite. Sadly, tick-borne diseases represent a serious public health crisis that will likely worsen over time, as the prevalence of tick-borne infections seems to be increasing.

This book by Karen Gloyer is one of the first of its kind to effectively teach children about the sinister behavior of ticks, the main transmitter of Lyme and a host of other pathogens. The book does a superb job of presenting vital information regarding early symptoms of Lyme in a child-friendly style. Ms. Gloyer's book covers practical prevention tools that a child can implement to protect him or herself against future tick bites. And the message is clear: Lyme is potentially very treatable when detected early!

Perhaps the most important thing I have learned over the years of working with Lyme patients is that *prevention* is the key. Avoidance, early detection, and treatment are all cornerstones of Lyme disease prevention. When practiced, avoidance, early detection and treatment can make all the difference in the world, and this is effectively illustrated in this educational book for children!

The first key prevention technique is *avoidance of tick contact*. Nick, the no good, icky tick comes to life in this book—yet he represents that there are no "good" ticks, that ticks are never our friends. Families can apply this principle by anticipating and evading tick infested areas, wearing protective clothing, using repellents (especially when going into the woods or tall grassy areas), not sleeping with pets, performing proper tick checks, and ensuring proper tick removal. These are all extremely useful and effective tools for avoiding Lyme disease and other tick-borne illnesses.

The second prevention method, *early detection,* can be very challenging for a couple of major reasons. First, many families are unaware of the signs and symptoms of Lyme disease. Additionally, Lyme, in its early stages, may be difficult to diagnose. The classic "bull's eye rash" is absolute proof of Lyme disease and, when present, no confirmation by blood-test is necessary. However, this classic rash is present *less than half the time*, making diagnosis quite difficult. Additionally, some Lyme-inexperienced medical practitioners refuse to treat a person with a classic rash unless the patient also presents with an abnormal Lyme blood test. However, the screening blood test for Lyme is very inaccurate and may misdiagnose Lyme over half the time, especially in the very early stages before a person's immune system has had time to produce a detectable blood-antibody response. Therefore, diagnosis can be challenging and prolonged. Author Karen Gloyer was improperly diagnosed for more than a decade! **The key lesson here is that all patients with a bull's eye rash should be treated for Lyme disease with an adequate course of antibiotics, *even if a tick was never seen, and even if Lyme blood tests are negative.***

The next challenge is finding an experienced medical doctor who understands tick-borne diseases, diagnosis, and treatment options. Without early diagnosis and treatment, Lyme can become a difficult, chronic disease. Most medical doctors are inadequately trained to properly handle complex cases of chronic Lyme disease. Fortunately, the most competent and best-trained Lyme doctors in the USA are usually members of an organization called the *International Lyme and Associated Diseases Society (ILADS)*. As a member myself, I endorse obtaining physician referral information from this organization. Their website is www.ilads.org.

Finally, given the growing problem of Lyme and other tick-borne illnesses, all of us parents, grandparents, and medical practitioners need to become very well-educated on this topic. We need to inform our families and neighbors about this growing menace. We need to educate people that we observe performing high risk behaviors in order to warn them about the dangers of ticks and Lyme disease. The days of innocent tick bites are over. We must become vigilant and engaged!

If there ever was truth to the old saying "an ounce of prevention is worth a pound of cure," it certainly applies to ticks and Lyme disease. Karen Gloyer's book certainly goes a long way toward educating the youngest among us about how to avoid this common and often debilitating condition called Lyme disease. As a former Lyme patient myself, I know the devastating effects of chronic, untreated Lyme. Having fully recovered, my medical practice is now devoted to helping other Lyme sufferers regain their health, their vitality, and their hope. To this end, I applaud Karen Gloyer for writing this book and being part of the solution!

> Kenneth B. Singleton, MD, MPH
> Author, *The Lyme Disease Solution*, and one of the leading physicians
> in the field of Lyme disease treatment and diagnosis

PREVENTION TIPS

AVOID CONTACT WITH TICKS

Prevention is key!
Anticipate and avoid tick-infested areas
Walk on cleared paths when possible
Wear protective clothing (i.e. shoes/socks, long pants/sleeves, hat, tie back long hair)
Use tick repellent, especially in woods or tall grassy areas
Use tick repellent on pets
Check pets for ticks soon after they have been outdoors
Avoid sleeping with pets who go outdoors
Keep yard free from tall grass, brush, leaves

EARLY DETECTION & REMOVAL

Lyme infection is less likely if a tick is attached for less than **36-48** hours. Early detection is key!
Shower and check for ticks soon after being outdoors (especially in wooded or tall grassy areas)
Check entire body (especially neck, head, scalp, ears, armpits, elbows, behind knees, groin, warm spots, belly button)
Use proper tick removal techniques
Save the tick in case it's needed for future TBD identification
Monitor for bull's eye rash (present only 50% of the time)
Recognize common symptoms of Lyme (i.e. fever, chills, fatigue, body aches, joint pain, swelling, headaches, may or may not be accompanied by bull's eye rash)

RAPID TREATMENT (following bulls-eye rash or symptoms)

If infected with Lyme, early diagnosis and treatment are key!
Seek Lyme treatment in the presence of symptoms, even if a tick was never seen or if blood tests are Lyme-negative. If you experience rash or fever, even weeks following a tick bite, seek medical attention from an experienced Lyme doctor (familiar with tick-borne diseases, diagnosis, treatment). Be sure to mention the tick bite. If bull's eye rash is present, always treat with antibiotics for Lyme.

EDUCATION

How could Nick, the no good, icky tick bite Abby and she not feel it? Tick bites are not painful and are easy to miss! Prevention, early detection and removal, and rapid treatment are key. Learn more about tick bites and Lyme disease using these resources recommended by Dr. Kenneth B. Singleton:

LYME INFORMATION WEBSITES

www.lymedoctor.com
www.lymedisease.org
www.lymediseaseassociation.org
www.lyme.org
www.lymeinfo.net
www.cdc.gov
www.columbia-lyme.org

ILADS (Lyme Physician Organization)

www.ilads.org

DOCTOR REFERRAL

www.lymediseaseassociation.org

LYME DISEASE FILM

www.openeyepictures.com

About the Author

Karen A. Gloyer's professional experience spans the fields of education, social work, human resources and recruiting. She earned a B.A. in Social Work (Memphis) as well as dual Master degrees in Social Work (Michigan) and Special Education (Fairfield University). Karen has served in leadership roles for the University of Michigan's Alumni Association in both Connecticut and Virginia. She has been recognized for her talents in military recruiting and awarded for her work with veterans and their families.

Karen's life took an unexpected turn when she started experiencing complicated, debilitating physical symptoms that remained undiagnosed for fourteen years. After more than a decade of hardship and pain, she was eventually diagnosed with Lyme disease and Babesia. Although she's learned how to weave life around Lyme, Karen's most recent teaching position at Lynnhaven Academy (Virginia) was cut short by a recurrence of the disease.

Karen's story is emblematic of the struggles too often accompanying Lyme diagnosis, as well as a testament to her tremendous resilience of spirit. Despite ongoing challenges, Karen remains passionate about educating children, families, and medical professionals about Lyme disease. She hopes that *Nick, the No Good, Icky Tick* will help others learn about Lyme disease and inspire prevention. Karen lives in Richmond, Virginia with her favorite four-footed friends, Chowser and Kelly, and her special two-footed love, Bill.

(Karen Gloyer pictured with Chowser, her 70-lb yellow lab/husky mix)

About the Illustrator

Maryana Kachmar was born in Lviv, Ukraine in 1983. She holds a Masters of Sacred Art from the National Academy of Arts in Lviv (Ukraine) and now participates in the artistic group, Zohrafos. Maryana has worked as editor and artist for several Christian children's magazines (including *Angelyatko* and *Flashlight*) and was chief artist and co-founder for a publishing company, Country of Angels. Over the last 10 years, she has illustrated more than 200 journals and 10 books, including numerous children's books (*ABC, Miracle in the Woods, Christmas,* and *Poems for Boys and Girls*). Fond of singing and making puppets, Maryana is the mother of two cheerful and energetic boys who inspire her daily with new pictures!